Dear Parent:

Buckle up! You are about to join your child on a very exciting journey. The destination? Independent reading!

Road to Reading will help you and your child get there. The program offers books at five levels, or Miles, that accompany children from their first attempts at reading to successfully reading on their own. Each Mile is paved with engaging stories and delightful artwork.

Getting Started
For children who know the alphabet and are eager to begin reading
• easy words • fun rhythms • big type • picture clues

Reading With Help
For children who recognize some words and sound out others with help
• short sentences • pattern stories • simple plotlines

Reading On Your Own
For children who are ready to read easy stories by themselves
• longer sentences • more complex plotlines • easy dialogue

First Chapter Books
For children who want to take the plunge into chapter books
• bite-size chapters • short paragraphs • full-color art

Chapter Books
For children who are comfortable reading independently
• longer chapters • occasional black-and-white illustrations

There's no need to hurry through the Miles. Road to Reading is designed without age or grade levels. Children can progress at their own speed, developing confidence and pride in their reading ability no matter what their age or grade.

So sit back and enjoy the ride—every Mile of the way!

Cover photography by: Tom Wolfson, Jennifer Hoon, James LaBianca, Steve Alfano, and Judy Tsuno

A GOLDEN BOOK • New York
Golden Books Publishing Company, Inc. New York, New York 10106

ISBN: 0-307-26328-2 (pbk)
ISBN: 0-307-46328-1 (GB)   A MM

barbie.com:
ballet buddies

by Barbara Richards
illustrated by S.I. International

Amy and Michelle loved ballet.

They took lessons

at Madame Margo's School of Dance.

Every Friday

the girls rode their bikes to class.

It was a hard ride.

The school was on a big hill.

"Come on, Michelle," yelled Amy.

"Madame Margo will be mad

if we are late."

"Madame Margo loves you,"

Michelle huffed,

trying to pedal faster.

"She will not be mad at you."

Amy and Michelle

raced into the classroom.

They were greeted by Madame Margo.

"Good afternoon, girls," she said.

Madame Margo gave Amy a smile.

"See what I mean?"

whispered Michelle.

Then Madame Margo clapped

her hands twice.

That meant she had something to say.

"In one month there will be

a big show," she said.

"We will dance to

The Magic Butterfly."

The whole class cheered.

"Everyone has an important part.

We will have lots of fairies,"

Madame said.

"And Amy will be our butterfly."

Michelle bit her lip.

She wished she could be the butterfly.

Still, Amy was a better dancer.

Michelle tried to be happy for her friend.

The next day Amy called Michelle.

"Want to come over?" she asked.

"We can practice for the show."

"Okay," said Michelle.

She hopped on her bike

and rode over to Amy's house.

First the girls danced Michelle's part.

One, two, three.

"Being a fairy is easy," said Michelle.

"You will be the prettiest fairy onstage,"

Amy told her friend.

Next the girls danced Amy's part.

One, two. One, two, three.

Slide! Leap! Twirl!

"Being a butterfly is hard," said Amy.

"Don't worry," said Michelle.

"I'll practice with you every day."

Soon it was one week

before the show.

After dance class, Amy was excited.

"Let's race!" she said.

The two friends rode their bikes,

down, down, down the big hill.

All of a sudden Amy's bike hit a rock.

She crashed into a bush.

"Are you okay?" asked Michelle.

Amy tried to stand up.

"My ankle!" she cried.

At the hospital the doctor
told Amy the bad news.
"Your ankle is broken," he said.
"You will have to wear a cast
for six weeks."
Now Amy could not dance in the show!

"Oh, dear!" cried Madame Margo
when she saw Amy's cast.
"We will need a new magic butterfly.
But who could learn the part
in less than a week?"

Just then Amy smiled.

"I've got it!" she said.

"Michelle knows the part.

She can be the magic butterfly!"

Madame Margo put her arm
around Michelle.

"Can you do it?" she asked.

"I—I—I think so," said Michelle.

Michelle wanted to dance the lead
more than anything.
But she was worried.
"What if I'm not good enough?"
she asked her friend.

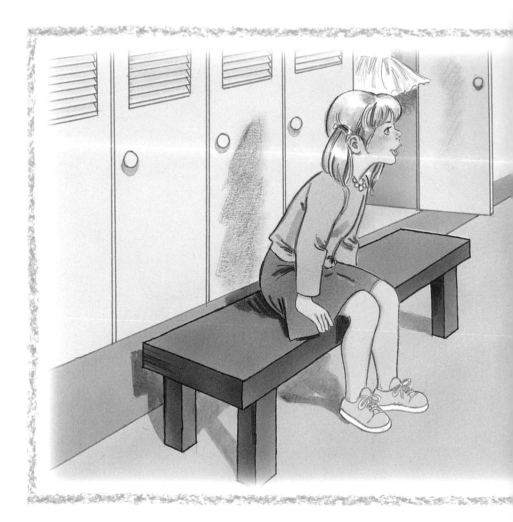

"I know!" said Amy.

"Let's go see Barbie.

She's a ballerina.

Maybe she can help."

"Great idea!" said Michelle.

At Michelle's house,

they turned on the computer.

Michelle typed *barbie.com.*

Before long the screen began to flash.

Light pink! Hot pink! Cotton-candy pink!

The computer screen began to grow.

Michelle helped Amy with her crutches.

Then the two girls stepped

through the pink fog.

"Hi, girls!" said a voice.

It was Barbie!

Barbie stared at Amy's cast.

"What happened?" she asked.

Amy told Barbie

how she fell off her bike.

And about the big show.

"Oh, Barbie," said Michelle.

"I need your help."

She told Barbie

that she was the butterfly now.

"We hoped you could give Michelle

some ballet tips," Amy added.

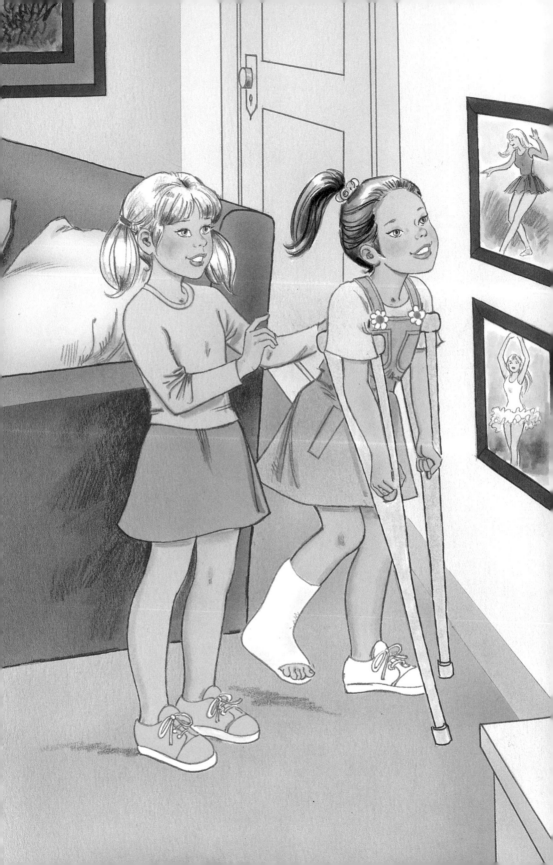

"I can try," said Barbie.

"I'll go change into my dance clothes."

Michelle and Amy waited

for Barbie in the den.

"Wow! It's Barbie dancing!"

said Michelle.

She pointed to some pictures

on the wall.

"Here's Barbie in *Swan Lake!*"

said Amy.

"And here she is in *The Nutcracker!*"

said Michelle.

Barbie poked her head into the room.

"Come on," she said, smiling.

In the living room,

Barbie had rolled back the rug

and moved the chairs.

"Our own stage," she told the girls.

Barbie and Michelle warmed up.

Then they began to dance.

"One, two. One, two, three,"

Barbie counted.

"Shoulders back. Point your toes,"

she said.

Barbie showed Michelle
how to hold her arms.
And how to keep her back straight.
"You are doing great!" said Barbie.

But Michelle was still worried.

"What if I mess up?" she asked.

Barbie gave her a hug.

"The most important thing,"

she said, "is to believe in yourself."

"Are you ever nervous

onstage, Barbie?" Amy asked.

Barbie sat down next to Amy.

"Sure," she said.

"I have butterflies in my stomach

before every show!

Once I was in *Sleeping Beauty*,"

Barbie went on.

"I was very nervous.

But then I started dancing

and having fun.

I forgot all about being scared."

"I wish I could get butterflies,"

Amy sighed.

She stared at her lumpy, white cast.

Michelle put her arm around her friend.

"I know something that might

cheer you up," said Barbie.

Barbie brought out a box

of magic markers.

She drew a pink butterfly

on Amy's cast.

Michelle drew a green butterfly.

Soon Amy's cast was
covered in butterflies.
Amy grinned.
"Thanks!" she said.

It was time to go home.

The girls begged Barbie

to come to the show.

"I will try," said Barbie,

turning on the computer.

Amy and Michelle hugged

Barbie good-bye.

"Thanks for everything,

Barbie!" they said.

Then they stepped into the pink fog.

In a moment, they were back

in Michelle's computer room.

"That was fun!" said Amy.

"Barbie is the best," agreed Michelle.

"I hope she can come to the show."

The next day Amy came

to Michelle's house.

"I have a surprise for you,"

Amy said.

She handed Michelle a present.

It was wrapped

in green tissue paper.

"Your ballet slippers!" said Michelle

when she opened the box.

"They're for good luck," said Amy.

Michelle gave Amy a big hug.

"Thanks," she said.

"But I am already lucky.

I am lucky to have you

as my best friend!"

Soon it was the night of the show.

Michelle peeked out

from behind the curtain.

Her parents were there

with her new baby sister.

So was Amy—right in the front row!

Michelle's stomach was full of butterflies.

But she remembered Barbie's words.

Have fun.

Always believe in yourself.

Michelle danced and twirled

around the stage.

Everyone cheered
at the end of the show.
Michelle grinned.
I wish Barbie could see me now,
she thought.
Then she took a bow.

That night Amy slept over
at Michelle's house.
"Let's play on the computer,"
said Michelle.
Suddenly the computer screen
began to blink.

A pair of pink ballet slippers
danced across the screen.

"It's a special message from Barbie!"
cried Michelle.

Great job! the message read.

The show really was magical!